Nora and the
Great Bear

Nora and the Great Bear

story and pictures by Ute Krause

* DIAL BOOKS FOR YOUNG READERS *
NEW YORK

Published by Dial Books for Young Readers
A Division of Penguin Books USA Inc.
2 Park Avenue
New York, New York 10016

Published simultaneously in Canada
by Fitzhenry & Whiteside Limited, Toronto
Copyright © 1989 by Ute Krause
All rights reserved
Printed in Hong Kong by South China Printing Co.
E
First Edition
1 3 5 7 9 10 8 6 4 2

Library of Congress Cataloging in Publication Data
Krause, Ute. Nora and the great bear.
Summary: Nora learns to hunt and dreams of capturing
the fabulous Great Bear, until she becomes lost in
the forest and it helps her.
[1. Bears—Fiction. 2. Hunting—Fiction.] I. Title.
PZ7.K8724No 1989 [Fic] 88-33538
ISBN 0-8037-0684-7
ISBN 0-8037-0685-5 (lib. bdg.)

The art for this book was prepared using black ink and watercolor.
It was then color-separated and reproduced
as red, blue, yellow, and black halftones.

Once in a tiny village near a great forest there lived a girl named Nora.

On long winter evenings when the snow lay in tall drifts around the houses, the villagers sat close together and told stories.

Sometimes they spoke of the Great Bear. Then a hush fell over the room. The villagers spoke in whispers, for it seemed as if the bear might be listening in the shadows.

"That bear is as old and as big as the forest itself," they said. "And it is fiercer and stronger than any other." They all were afraid of it but each of them dreamed of being the one to capture it.

After listening to many stories about the Great Bear, Nora was curious.

"Will the person who finds it be the greatest bear hunter of all?" she asked.

"Yes, indeed!" answered Jake, one of the hunters. "Are you going to try?"

"I think I will," said Nora.

"You're too small to be a bear hunter," said the others, laughing. "And way too frail!"

Nora scowled and said firmly, "I'll be the best bear hunter of all."

She worked at becoming strong and practiced with her
bow and arrow until she could hit a bull's-eye blindfolded.

Finally the day came when Nora was allowed
to join the village hunters. Early one morning in
fall, when the mist was still rising between the trees,
they set off on their annual search for the Great Bear.

They traveled deep into the forest, and by nightfall they found a clearing where they set up their camp.

"Tell me some more stories about the Great Bear," said Nora, and the hunters told their tales far into the night.

When she fell asleep, Nora dreamed of bringing home the Great Bear herself, and of how the villagers would line the streets and shout "Hurray!" as she went by.

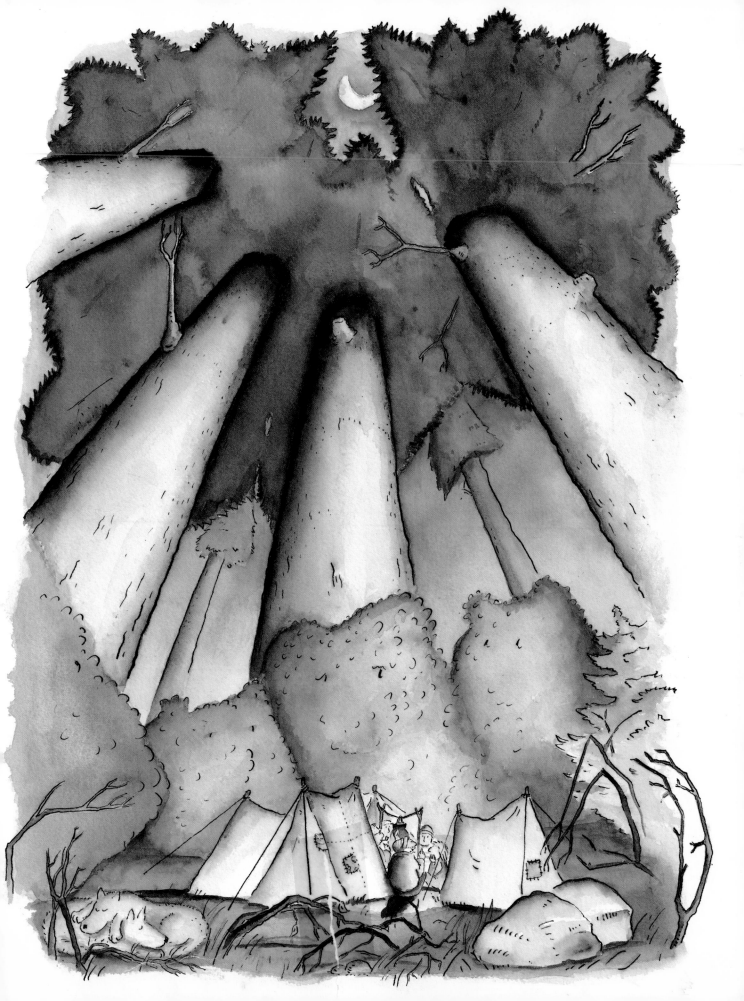

The next morning before the gray dawn Nora and the
villagers set out to hunt the Great Bear. Nora learned how
to build traps, but the Great Bear never came near them.

She became a fast runner, quick to follow the dogs, but they never led her to any bear tracks.

She learned to be patient, as she crouched quietly with the hunters, listening. Many animals came by and Nora learned to recognize their sounds, but the bear was not among them.

She learned to hunt upwind and to keep a sharp lookout for tracks, until she was better than anyone at finding them. She learned to find her way around the forest, until she felt at home in it.

Every day she went out to search for the Great Bear
until it seemed as if *it* were watching *her*, but there was never
a sign of it.

"I'm sure it's somewhere close by here," she said.

"Perhaps," said Jake.

"Then *why* can't we see it!" Nora asked, but Jake just
shrugged and shook his head.

The chill of winter filled the air and the hunters began
to talk of returning home. Nora listened sadly.

"I so wanted to find the bear," she sighed.

"Maybe we'll have better luck next year," the others said.

Nora said nothing but hunched her shoulders and wandered off.
Everything that she had learned about hunting the bear had been of
no use. She sat down to think about it and then suddenly she knew.
It was so simple!

   She tied up the dogs and put down her weapons. "Can I see
you now, bear?" she called into the forest. But there was no reply, so
Nora set off among the trees.

It began to snow. As she walked further and further into the forest, Nora thought she could feel the bear close beside her. And then she saw the track. There could be no doubt. It was a bear's claw-marked footprint. And over there was another and another still. Her heart thundered so loudly, she was sure that the bear could hear it.

On and on she followed the tracks leading into a part of the forest where she had never been before.

The sun began to set and still the bear was nowhere in sight.
Darkness came and the snow continued to fall. The bear was nowhere
to be seen. At last Nora gave up and turned back. But when she
tried to retrace her steps, the snow had completely covered them.
She was lost.

Cold and hungry, she leaned against a
tree. She had never felt so alone. The forest
stretched out forever on all sides. How she
wished she had never gone bear hunting!

The snow stopped and as she looked
up, she saw a shadow fall between the trees.
It was...

the Great Bear.

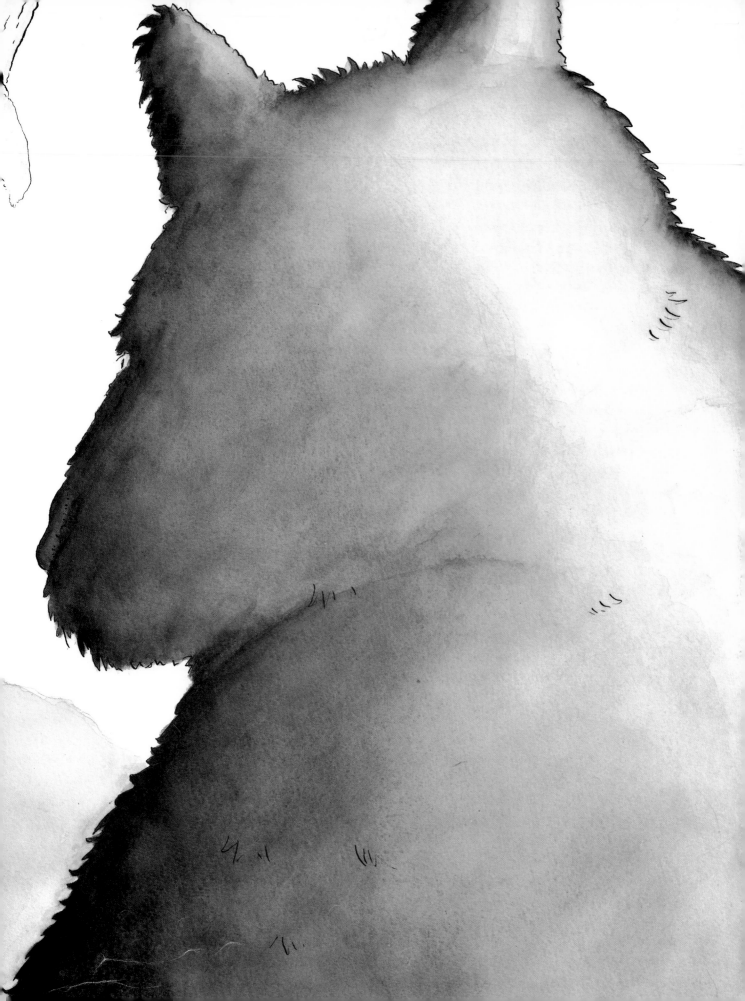

It even hid the moon as it loomed over her, bigger than she had ever imagined. Nora held her breath. She had never been so scared in all her life.

The bear looked at her and its eyes glowed in the moonlight. Nora gathered up her courage and looked back. And the longer she looked at the bear, the less afraid she grew. Instead, she saw how beautiful it was.

She stretched out a hand to touch it, but the bear dropped on all fours and trotted away.

Then it stopped and waited.

"Are you waiting for me," asked Nora. Slowly she came closer and again the bear moved a few paces away. She followed and in silence they went on and on through the night.

At last she saw a light in the distance. It was the camp! Happily she turned toward the bear, but it was gone. Except for her own footprints the snow was untouched.

The hunters were so relieved to see her that they forgot to be angry with her for going off alone. A warm meal was soon made and she was given so many bear hugs that she almost had her breath squeezed out of her.

"Where have you been?" asked Jake.

"Bear hunting."

"And did you find a bear?"

"Yes," said Nora proudly, "I found the Great Bear.

The hunters chuckled. "Well, what was it like?"

"As old and as big as the forest," said Nora with a smile. "And just as beautiful!"

And as she looked into the forest that night, she was sure she could see the Great Bear moving through the moonlight.